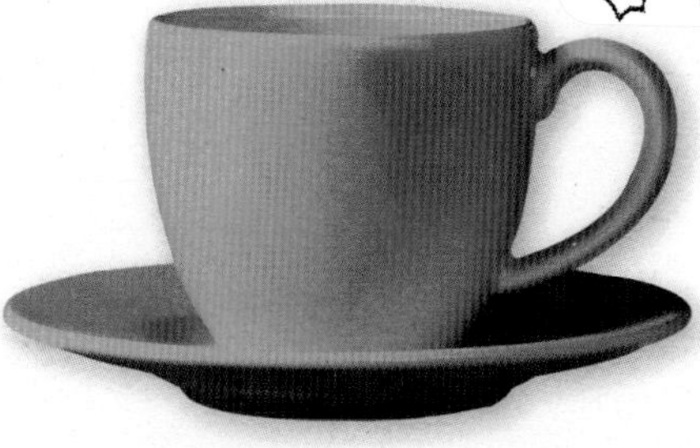

Plain AND Fancy

by Jennifer Kandoian

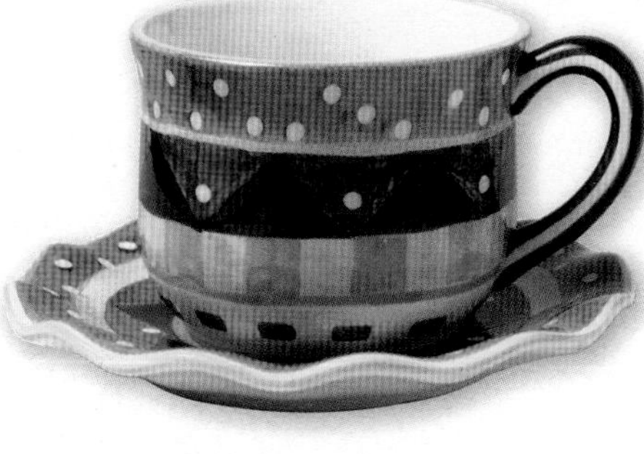

HOUGHTON MIFFLIN BOSTON

To the Teacher

This wordless book focuses on developing vocabulary for describing words such as *plain* and *fancy.*

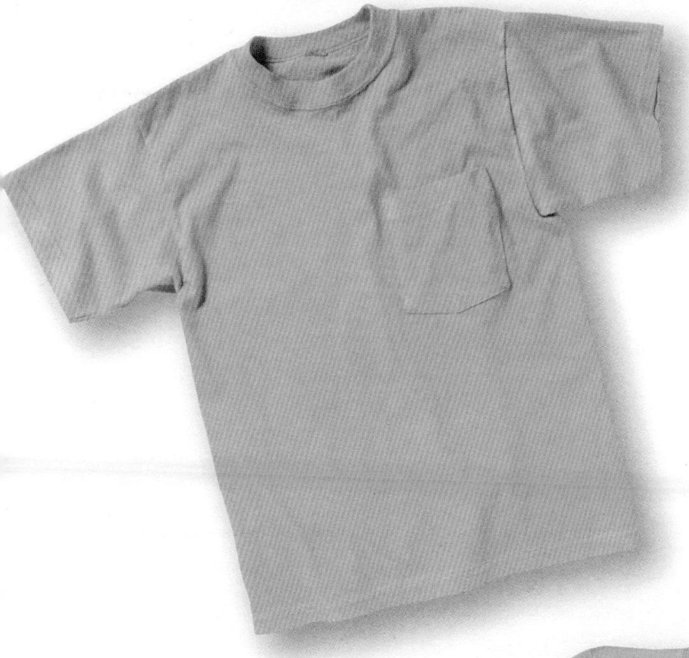

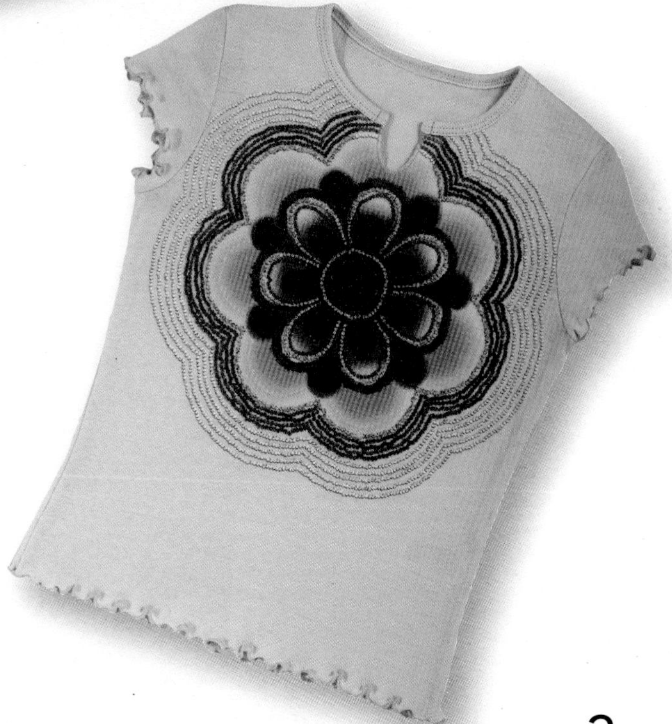

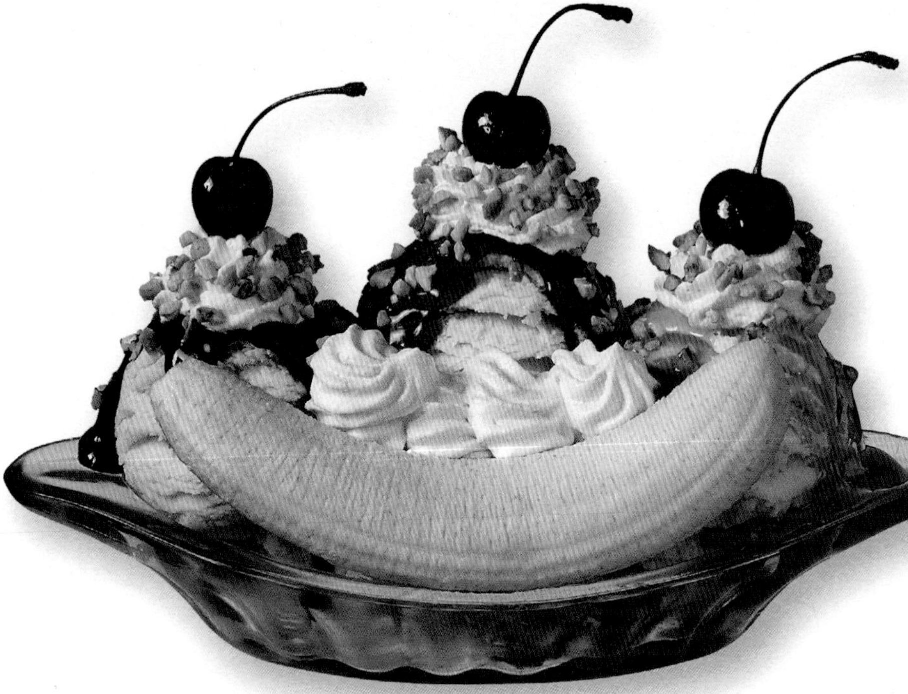

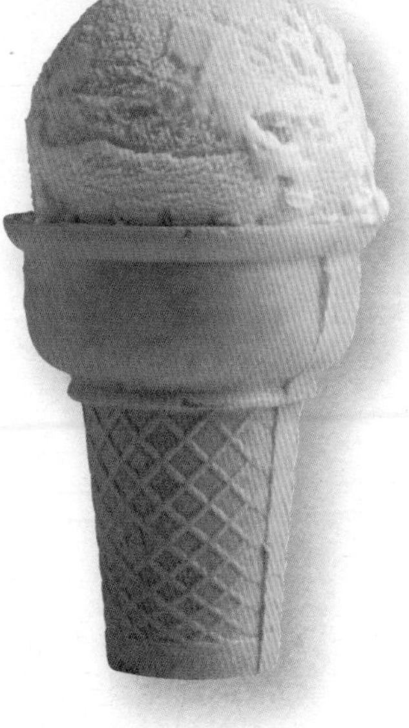

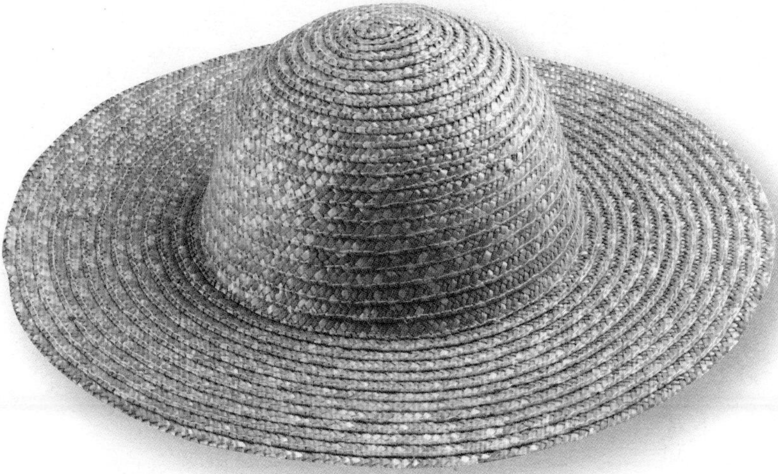

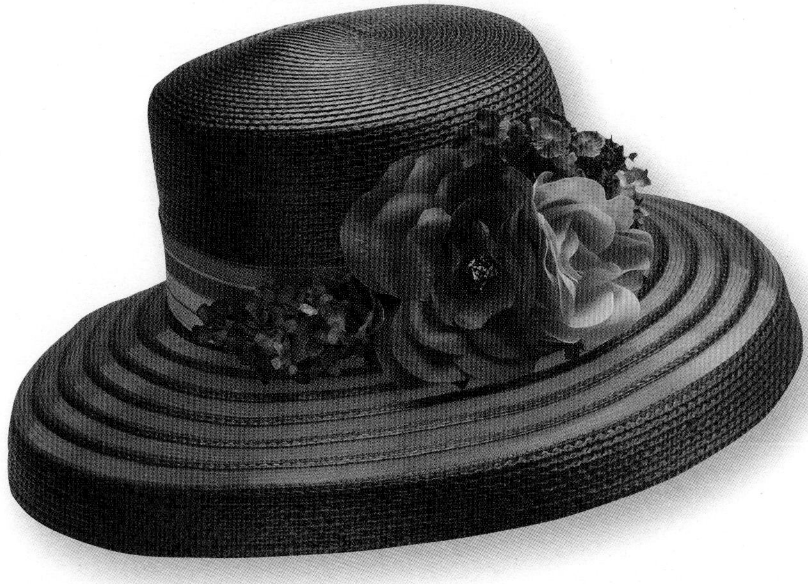

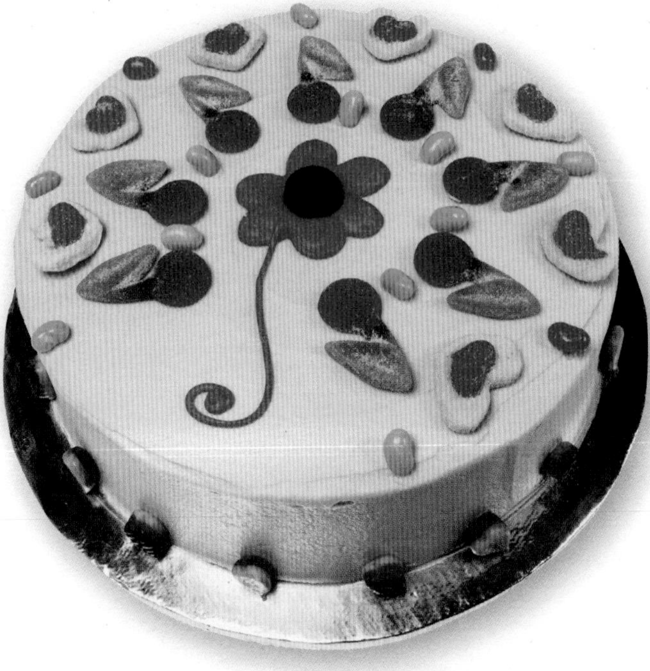

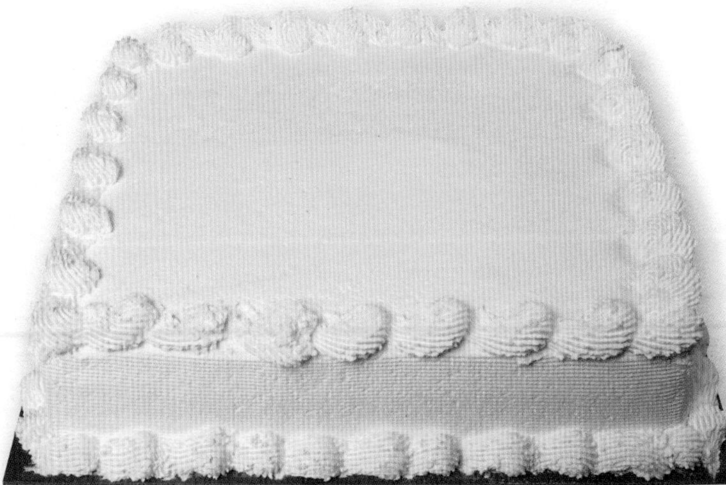

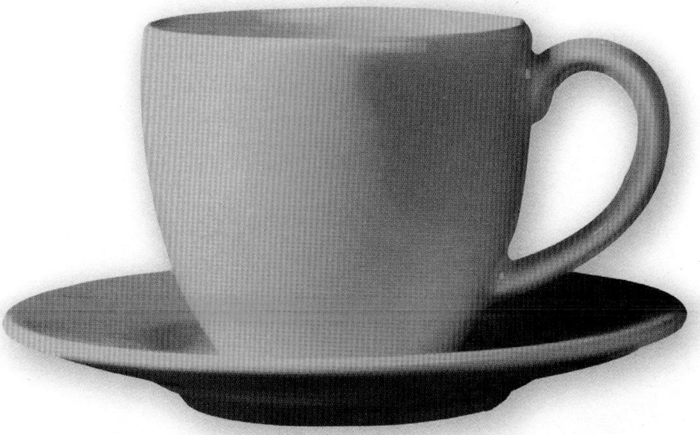

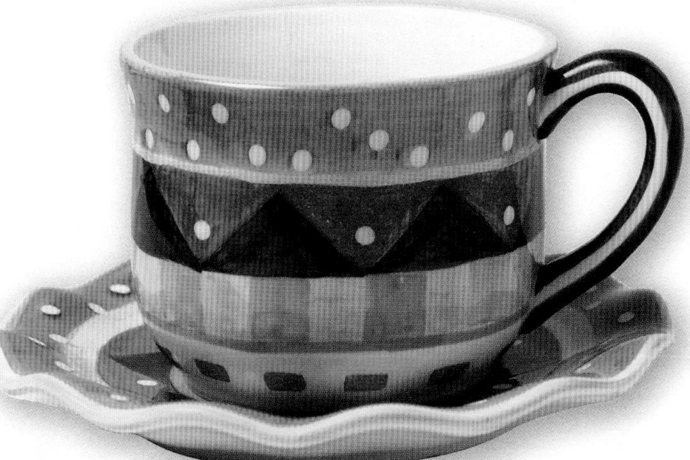

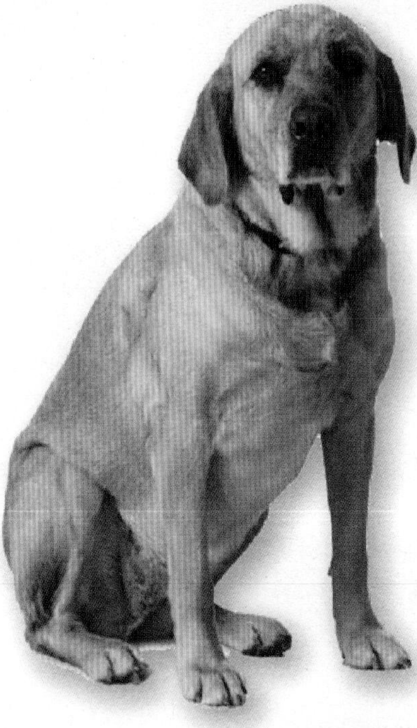

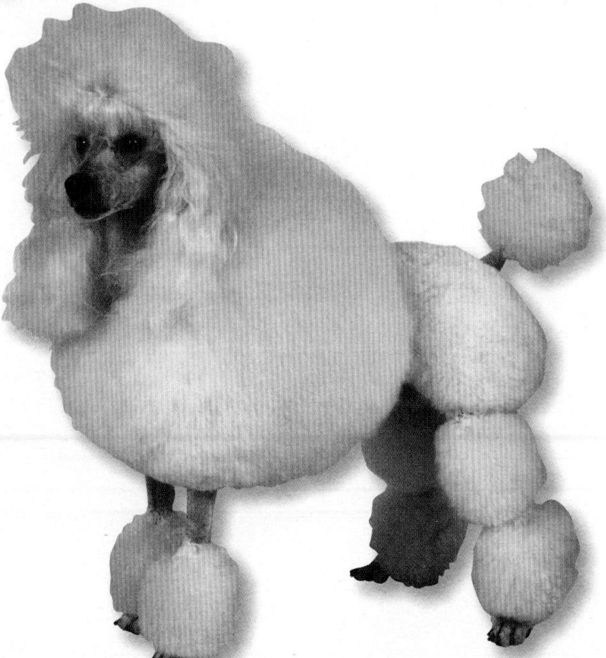